Sport

KU-386-003

Little Joe's
Big Race

First published in 2000 by
Franklin Watts
96 Leonard Street
London
EC2A 4XD

Franklin Watts Australia
14 Mars Road
Lane Cove
NSW 2066

A CIP catalogue record for this book is available
from the British Library.

ISBN 0 7496 3712 9

Series Editor: Louise John
Series Advisor: Dr Barrie Wade
Series Designer: Jason Anscomb

Printed in Hong Kong

For Verona – A.B

Little Joe's Big Race

by Andy Blackford

Illustrated by Tim Archbold

W
FRANKLIN WATTS
NEW YORK • LONDON • SYDNEY

Little Joe didn't like Sports Day.

He was so little, a frog
could jump higher.

He was so slow, a tortoise
could run faster.

But Little Joe was good
at balancing things.

He decided to win
the egg and spoon race.

9

And Little Joe did win!

But he was so excited,
he forgot to stop.

He ran out of the
school gates ...

... and through the town.

He ran all day ...

... and all night too.

He swam through rivers.

He ran up ...

... and down mountains.

One day, there was a
loud CRACK!

Out of the egg popped
a chicken.

Still Joe kept running.

He ran through the sun ...

... and through the rain.

Soon, the chicken grew
too big for the spoon.

Little Joe had to carry
him on a spade.

At the same time,
Little Joe grew bigger
and bigger.

One year later, Little Joe arrived back at school.

It was Sports Day again.
Everyone was cheering.

"Well done, Big Joe!"
cried the teacher.

"You've won the chicken and spade race!"

And she gave Joe and
the chicken a medal.

Leapfrog has been specially designed to fit the requirements of the
National Literacy Strategy. It offers real books for beginning readers
by top authors and illustrators.

There are five other humorous stories to choose from:

The Bossy Cockerel   **ISBN 0 7946 3708 0**

Written by **Margaret Nash**, illustrated by **Elisabeth Moseng**

A traditional farmyard story with a twist. Charlie the Cockerel is very bossy indeed.
The hens think it's time he got his come-uppance ...

Bill's Baggy Trousers   **ISBN 0 7496 3709 9**

Written by **Susan Gates**, illustrated by **Anni Axworthy**

A frivolous fantasy story about Bill and his new, baggy trousers, which turn out to be a lot
more fun than he could have imagined!

The Cheeky Monkey   **ISBN 0 7496 3710 2**

Written by **Anne Cassidy**, illustrated by **Lisa Smith**

A hilarious story about a little girl with a vivid imagination who encounters a
monkey hiding in her treehouse. Read all about the exploits of Wendy as she tries to make the
mischievous monkey leave.

Mr Spotty's Potty   **ISBN 0 7496 3711 0**

Written by **Hilary Robinson**, illustrated by **Peter Utton**

A rhyming text with repetitive and patterned language about Mr Spotty's attempts to grow seeds
in an old potty. It soon becomes clear that Dot, his dog, may be the reason behind his success.

The Little Star   **ISBN 0 7496 3713 7**

Written by **Deborah Nash**, illustrated by **Richard Morgan**

A fantasy story with an element of humour about a little star who no longer wants to live in
the sky. His friend, the Moon, takes him on a magical journey to show him how much fun the
sky can be.